This book belongs to
Lindsay Bull

Bluebell Glade

Dandelion Dell

Heart of Misty Wood

Hawthorn Hedgerows

Heather Hill

Sundown Hill

Crystal Cave

Golden Meadow

Moonshine Pond

Dewdrop Spring

Honeydew Meadow

Mulberry Bushes

Misty Wood Rabbit Warren

HOME SWEET HOME

How many Fairy Animals books have you collected?

- ✓ Chloe the Kitten
- ✓ Bella the Bunny
- ✓ Paddy the Puppy
- ✓ Mia the Mouse
- ✓ Poppy the Pony
- ✓ Hailey the Hedgehog

And there are more magical adventures coming very soon!

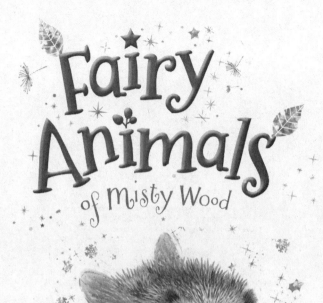

Fairy Animals
of Misty Wood

Hailey the Hedgehog

Lily Small

Henry Holt and Company
New York

With special thanks to Liss Norton

Henry Holt and Company, LLC
Publishers since 1866
175 Fifth Avenue
New York, New York 10010
mackids.com

First published in the United States in 2016 by Henry Holt and Company, LLC.
Originally published in Great Britain in 2013 by Egmont UK Limited.

Library of Congress Cataloging-in-Publication Data
Names: Small, Lily, author.
Title: Hailey the Hedgehog / Lily Small.
Description: First American Edition. | New York : Henry Holt and Company, 2016. |
Series: Fairy animals of misty wood | Summary: "A special story for Christmas
introducing Hailey the Hedgerow Hedgehog, the newest addition to the Fairy
Animals of Misty Wood"—Provided by publisher.
Identifiers: LCCN 2015050734 (print) | LCCN 2016023317 (ebook) | ISBN 9781627797351
(paperback) | ISBN 9781627797368 (Ebook)
Subjects: | CYAC: Fairies—Fiction. | Hedgehogs—Fiction. | Forest animals—Fiction. |
Christmas—Fiction. | BISAC: JUVENILE FICTION / Fantasy & Magic. | JUVENILE
FICTION / Social Issues / Friendship.
Classification: LCC PZ7.S6385 Hai 2016 (print) | LCC PZ7.S6385 (ebook) |
DDC [Fic]—dc23
LC record available at https://lccn.loc.gov/2015050734

Our books may be purchased in bulk for promotional, educational, or business use.
Please contact your local bookseller or the Macmillan Corporate
and Premium Sales Department at (800) 221-7945 ext. 5442
or by e-mail at MacmillanSpecialMarkets@macmillan.com.

First American Edition—2016
Printed in the United States of America by
R. R. Donnelley & Sons Company, Harrisonburg, Virginia

1 3 5 7 9 10 8 6 4 2

Contents

CHAPTER ONE

Parade Day!

Winter had come to Misty Wood, and the fairy animals were very excited—today was the day of the Christmas Parade!

Hailey, a tiny hedgehog, lay in her cozy bed of moss, listening to the wind outside singing through the trees. She pulled her blanket of velvety dock leaves up to her nose.

"I do love winter," Hailey said with a sigh. As she pictured the wind blowing the last of the golden leaves from the branches and the woods twinkling with frost, she started to smile.

"Are you up, Hailey?" her dad

called from the far end of their
burrow.

"Nearly," Hailey called back.
She jumped out of bed, licked her
tiny pink paws, and gave her face
a quick wash. Then she checked her
dandelion clock. "Yay!" she cried.
"It's breakfast time!"

When she got to the other
end of the burrow, her dad was
busy chopping acorns. "Morning,
Hailey," he said. "I'm making

3

you some acorn porridge to keep you nice and warm out there. The woods are going to need a lot of tidying up before the parade."

"Great!" Hailey exclaimed. "I love having lots of leaves to collect." She fluttered her silver-and-red wings excitedly, sending sparkles of glittering light around the burrow.

Hailey was a Hedgerow Hedgehog. Like all the other fairy animals, she had a special job

to do to help make Misty Wood
a wonderful place to live. The
Hedgerow Hedgehogs' job was to
collect fallen leaves on their prickly
spines, to keep the woods neat
and tidy. That was why Hailey
loved winter so much. There were
so many colorful leaves to gather,
especially on a windy day like this.

Dad finished making the
porridge and poured it into three
nutshell bowls. Hailey took hers

and went to sit on a pebble stool in the corner. Just as she ate her first mouthful, a gust of cold air came whisking through the burrow.

"It's only me," a voice called. Hailey's mom hurried inside. Her paws were full of mistletoe sprigs. "Goodness!" she exclaimed. "What a wind!" Laying the mistletoe on the conker table, she smoothed down the ruffled fur on her face and legs.

7

"Ooh, is the mistletoe for the Christmas Parade?" Hailey asked. She could hardly wait for the parade to start. It took place every year. All the fairy animals dressed up in beautiful leaves and berries and marched through Misty Wood behind the Moss Mouse pipe-and-drum band. Afterward, everyone visited the nests and burrows of their friends to admire their decorations and to share a tasty

8

nibble or an acorn cup of warm
cranberry juice.

"Yes," her mom replied. "I'm
using mistletoe and holly this year."
She turned around, and Hailey saw
that her mom's prickles were stuck
all over with shiny red holly berries.

"I'll string them together
to make garlands," her mom
continued. She shook the berries
from her spines and pushed them
into a tidy pile beside the fire.

9

Hailey couldn't stop smiling
as she pictured herself wearing a
beautiful red-and-white garland. In
fact, she was grinning so much that
some porridge trickled out of the
corner of her mouth! Hailey quickly

licked it up with her velvety pink tongue.

"Here's your breakfast," said Hailey's dad, passing her mom a bowl of porridge. "And I'm making my special chestnut pudding for after the parade."

"Yippee!" Hailey cheered. That was another good thing about winter—there were always chestnuts to be found, and Dad's chestnut pudding was *delicious*!

11

Hailey ate her porridge quickly. Every day she made sure that Misty Wood was spick-and-span, but today—parade day—she was determined to be extra careful. Today, she wouldn't leave a single leaf out of place. And she had to make sure she got home earlier than usual, too, so she'd have time to dress up.

"I'm off, then," she said as soon as her bowl was empty.

"Don't forget that the parade begins at one o'clock, Hailey," her mom reminded her.

"I won't," Hailey said with a smile. There was *no way* she was going to miss her favorite event!

Spreading her wings, she fluttered up the long passageway that led out of her warm burrow and into Hawthorn Hedgerows, which grew at the very edge of Misty Wood.

As soon as Hailey got above ground she could see that the wind had been busy. Only a few leaves still clung to the twigs above her head. They fluttered as the wind danced around them, whistling its winter tune.

They'll be off soon, too, thought Hailey, smiling. *And then I'll have even more leaves to tidy.*

She flitted out from under the hedgerow and gasped in delight.

Jack Frost had been at work during the night, sprinkling his glittering ice crystals across the grass. The crystals shimmered pink, blue, and silver in the wintry sunshine, and each blade of grass stood up stiff and straight no matter how hard the wind blew.

Hailey gazed around. *"Beautiful,"* she breathed. She fluttered up into the air and spread her wings wide so the wind would lift her high. She

wanted to look at the grassy spaces
between the hedgerows. "I'll start
collecting leaves in the messiest
patch," she said to herself.

Up, up, up she soared into
the clear blue sky. Soon, Misty

16

Wood was spread out beneath her like a colorful patchwork quilt. The frosted grass glinted silver. Dewdrop Spring was the same bright blue as the sky, with spots of shiny ice here and there. And the

17

patch of snowdrops beside it looked as clean and white as a fluffy cloud.

Farther on still, Moonshine Pond shone pearly blue, full of glowing moonbeams, and beyond that was the pretty, vivid purple of Heather Hill.

Right in the center of it all was a patch of deep, dark green—the mysterious Heart of Misty Wood, where the Wise Wishing Owl lived.

Hailey had never seen the Wise
Wishing Owl, but she had heard
lots of stories about her wisdom.
And everyone said that she had the
power to grant wishes.

As Hailey looked around, she
spotted a patch of leaf-strewn grass
not far from her burrow. She quickly
fluttered down. "Perfect!" she cried
happily, puffing out her spikes.
"Now I'm ready to start work!"

Hungry Hugo!

Tucking her nose and legs in
against her tummy and folding
her glittering wings, Hailey curled
herself into a tight ball. Then she

rolled to and fro across the frosty
grass, gathering the leaves on her
prickles.

Soon the patch of grass was
clear. Hailey scurried over to a

21

nearby hedge and shook herself. The leaves fluttered down from her spines, and she scooped them into a tidy heap at the base of the hedge. Smiling, she looked across the spotless grass. "Good job!" she congratulated herself. "Now on to the next one."

She unfurled her wings and flew farther into the woods.

Soon, she came to a grove where the Holly Hamsters were

hard at work. They were nibbling the glossy holly leaves into their beautiful curved shapes.

"Hello, Holly Hamsters!" Hailey called as she fluttered past.

"Hello, Hailey!" they called back, their chubby cheeks bulging.

Just beyond the holly grove was an ancient chestnut tree with twisted branches and a huge, fat trunk. Leaves were scattered around it, and Hailey eagerly

23

swooped down to gather them
all up.

As she rolled to and fro,
collecting the leaves, she made
up a little song:

> *I love winter when the wild wind*
>> *blows,*
>
> *Scattering the leaves all around,*
>> *all around,*
>
> *Even though it chills my nose*
>> *and toes,*
>
> *When I roll on the frosty ground.*

Suddenly, she heard a small voice. "I hate winter," it said. "I don't know why you're singing about it. It's the worst season of the whole year!"

Hailey stopped rolling and uncurled herself. She looked around in surprise. How could anybody hate winter?

A teeny-tiny Holly Hamster with pale brown fur and yellow wings was crouched on the edge of

the holly grove. His head and wings were drooping miserably. Hailey recognized him—it was Hugo.

"Whatever's the matter, Hugo?" asked Hailey.

"I've ruined my holly bush," he replied, looking up sadly. "And now it's going to look horrible for the Christmas Parade. Every fairy animal in the whole wood will march past here and see what I've done."

Hailey fluttered over to him.

"Perhaps it's not as bad as you . . ."
She fell silent as she spotted the
bush. "Oh, dear."

The bush was almost
completely bare, with every leaf
nibbled right down to the stem.

Hailey stared at Hugo. "What happened to it?"

"I was hungry," Hugo said. "And the leaves were so yummy I couldn't stop eating them." He peered up at Hailey dreamily. "Honestly, they were the most delicious things I've ever tasted—even more delicious than chestnuts!" He sat back on the ground and gave a loud burp.

Hailey's tummy rumbled as

28

she thought of her dad's chestnut pudding. It was hard to imagine anything tasting nicer. They must have been very tasty leaves indeed!

"Maybe I should try digging up the whole bush," Hugo said. "Then I could hide it." The tiny hamster leaped up and began scratching at the soil around the bush's roots.

"No, Hugo!" Hailey cried. "Don't do that." She rubbed her

29

nose thoughtfully. "I think I know what to do," she said at last.

Hugo looked at her hopefully, his dark eyes shining. "Really?"

"Wait here a moment," said Hailey. She fluttered back to the chestnut tree and quickly rolled over the last of the leaves to stick them to her prickles. Then she whooshed back to Hugo.

"Here you go," she said, shaking the leaves to the ground.

"You can nibble these into holly leaf shapes, and I'll hang them on the bush."

Hugo bounced up and down on his hind legs. "That's brilliant! Thanks, Hailey!" he cried.

"Just make sure you don't gobble them all up this time," Hailey said with a grin.

"I won't," Hugo said, patting his furry tummy. "I'm far too full!" Then he set to work, taking dainty

little bites out of the edges of the bright chestnut tree leaves.

Hailey twisted the leaf stems around the holly twigs and soon the bush was covered in golden holly-shaped leaves.

"These leaves make my bush look so pretty!" Hugo cried out happily. He hugged Hailey, then leaped back. "Ouch! I forgot all about your prickles!" He chuckled, rubbing his paws.

"Sorry," giggled Hailey. "But I'm glad you're pleased with your *holly* bush."

"I am!" Hugo exclaimed. Then he looked at the little pile of spare leaves next to him. "Can you close

your eyes for a minute?" he asked
Hailey.

"Why?" Hailey said, puzzled.

"I can't tell you yet—it's a
surprise."

Hailey loved surprises. She
closed her eyes and listened, trying
to work out what Hugo was doing.
But all she could hear was the
rustle of leaves.

"Ta-da!" cried Hugo after a
few minutes.

Hailey opened her eyes.

"I made this just for you," Hugo said. He held up a beautiful garland made from all the spare leaves. He slipped it over Hailey's head. "It's to say thank you for helping me."

"It's lovely!" Hailey exclaimed. "Thanks, Hugo. I'll wear it in the Christmas Parade. Ooh, I'd better get going—I've got loads of work to do before then!"

CHAPTER THREE

A Shimmer of Moonbeams

Hailey soared into the air and fluttered quickly over the rabbit warren. Down below, her friend

Bella the Bud Bunny was hard at work opening snowdrop buds with her twitchy nose. Hailey waved, but she didn't fly down to speak to Bella in case it made her late for the parade.

38

She flew over Dewdrop Spring, then on to Moonshine Pond, which shone like a blue pearl in the winter sunshine. "Ha!" she cried as she spotted some leaves at the pond's edge.

Hailey flew down to land. She curled into a ball and rolled quickly down the bank, gathering the leaves on her prickles as she went. She sang her song as she rolled faster and faster:

I love winter when the wild wind

blows,

Scattering the leaves all around,

all around,

Even though it chills my nose

and toes,

When I roll on the frosty ground.

"I used to love winter, but I most definitely don't anymore!" said a gloomy voice.

The voice was coming from a tall pine tree beside the pond.

Hailey unrolled quickly, and looked around in surprise. "Who said that?" she asked.

"Me, Maisie the Moonbeam Mole," the voice replied softly.

Hailey was very puzzled indeed. Moonbeam Moles didn't usually come out during the day. They did their special job at nighttime— catching moonbeams and scattering them in Moonshine Pond to make it look pearly and beautiful. During

the day they stayed in their burrows and slept—and they certainly didn't go climbing trees! Hailey knew that they woke up specially for the Christmas Parade each year—but it was a bit too early yet.

Hailey fluttered over quickly to investigate.

A pair of tiny brown eyes peeked out from among the pine needles. They looked very tired and were full of tears.

"What's wrong, Maisie?" Hailey gasped. "And why are you still awake?"

"I've been here since last night." Maisie sniffed sadly. "My net's caught in this tree, and I can't pull it free." She crept along a branch and pointed up to the top of the tree with a trembling paw.

Hailey saw something glowing among the branches. It was the net—crammed full of twinkling

43

moonbeams. It had gotten tangled around some pinecones.

"I can't put my moonbeams into the pond"—Maisie gulped—"so it won't look lovely for the Christmas Parade."

"But it *does* look lovely," Hailey told her. "I noticed it when I was flying this way. It looks like a beautiful pearl." She flew up and patted the tiny mole's shoulder, trying to make her feel better.

45

"Not my bit of the pond," sobbed Maisie. She pointed to a patch of water close to the bank. Now Hailey understood why Maisie was so upset. The water there was dark and still, with not even a hint of glistening moonlight.

Hailey thought hard. "I know what to do!" she cried. "I'll hook my prickles through your net. Then I'll be able to fly up and lift it clear of those pinecones."

Maisie stopped crying and gazed hopefully at Hailey. "Do you think it will work?" she whispered.

"There's only one way to find out," said Hailey.

She soared to the top of the tree, then fluttered around it, hooking the net over her prickles. "Here goes," she called. Flapping her wings hard, she flew higher still. Part of the net came free and some pinecones dropped to the ground.

"It's working!" squealed Maisie happily.

Hailey flapped her wings harder than ever. More pinecones dropped down and now most of the net was free. "One more try," Hailey panted. Using all of her strength, she zoomed into the air and suddenly the net was dangling free below her. The moonbeams twinkled as they swung from side to side.

"Hurray!" Hailey cheered. She flew to the ground with the heavy net.

Maisie fluttered down beside her, her lilac wings shimmering in the sunshine. "Thank you, thank you," she cried. Her tiny eyes shone with relief as she unhooked the net from Hailey's spines. "Now the pond will look perfect for the parade!"

Scooping out a pawful of

moonbeams, Maisie tossed them into the patch of dark water. They plopped down out of sight, then rose to the surface and their beautiful pearly light rippled out, making the water gleam.

"That looks beautiful, Maisie," breathed Hailey, flying up to see the pond from above.

"All because of you," replied Maisie. She reached into her net and took out the last glowing

moonbeam. "May I give you a
present to thank you for helping
me?" she asked shyly.

51

"Oh yes, please!" Hailey cried. She loved presents!

Maisie placed the moonbeam on the biggest leaf in Hailey's garland. Hailey watched entranced as gold and silver sparkles spread from leaf to leaf. Soon the whole garland was twinkling brightly.

"Thank you!" gasped Hailey, astonished. She'd never seen anything so beautiful before. It was as though she were wearing

a necklace made of glittering

moonlight.

"No, thank *you*, Hailey,"

Maisie said. "If you hadn't helped

me, the pond wouldn't have looked

its best for the Christmas Parade today."

"The parade!" Hailey cried, remembering how much she had to do before it began. "I must go! Bye, Maisie."

CHAPTER FOUR

A Starry Surprise

Hailey fluttered up into the air and
headed for the trees that grew in
the Heart of Misty Wood. She could
see a few untidy leaves on the grass

there. As she drew near, she started to sing her winter song:

I love winter when the wild wind

blows—

"Well, I don't!" boomed a cross voice. It was coming from behind a tree at the very back of the Heart of Misty Wood.

Hailey peeped around the tree trunk nervously, wondering who it could be.

Boris, one of the Bark Badgers,

was hunched on the frosty ground.
He was frowning at his paw.

"What's wrong, Boris?" Hailey
asked. The Bark Badgers carved
beautiful patterns into tree trunks
with their strong claws. They were
usually very kind and helpful.
Hailey had never seen one looking
so grumpy before.

"I'm supposed to be carving
wintry patterns into the bark of the
trees around here," Boris replied.

"I wanted everything to be perfect for the parade, so I flew up onto a branch to reach farther up the trunk. But the branch was slippery with frost and I fell down." He held up his paw and Hailey saw that it was sore and swollen. "Now my paw's so painful that I can't do my job," he sighed.

"Poor you," Hailey said. She wondered what she could do to help him.

"I should have been more careful!" Boris said glumly. "Now when the parade comes past here, the fairy animals won't be thinking happy, Christmassy thoughts.

They'll be thinking, look at those plain old trees!"

Suddenly, they heard some loud barking and looked around, startled. A group of Pollen Puppies came scampering along, their ears flopping and their tongues hanging out with excitement. "Hey! Aren't you coming to the Christmas Parade?" the puppies woofed, wagging their tails and scattering specks of golden pollen all around.

"Is it time?" Hailey asked them anxiously.

"Nearly," one of the puppies woofed. "And we don't want to be late!"

"Neither do I!" Hailey gulped as the playful pups went bounding away. Her mind started whirring. She couldn't leave poor Boris looking so unhappy. Maybe she could help him *and* make it back home in time for the start of the parade. . . .

"Let me help," Hailey said. "My spines are nearly as sharp as a badger's claws. If you tell me what to do, perhaps I can carve the tree trunks for you."

Boris's face broke into a cheery smile. "That would be wonderful!" he exclaimed.

Hailey flew up and pressed her prickles against the first tree. "Okay, I'm ready," she said. "Tell me what to do."

"Go up a bit," called Boris.

Hailey fluttered upward. She felt her spines cutting through the tree's bark. "I think it's working!" she cried excitedly.

"Now right a bit," Boris said, beaming.

Hailey flew right.

"Left, then down," called Boris.

Hailey followed all of Boris's instructions.

"That's it," he said at last. "The first tree's finished. Let's see if it worked."

Hailey turned to look at the tree trunk. "Oh!" she gasped. "How pretty!" Her spines had carved a

A STARRY SURPRISE

pattern of beautiful lacy snowflakes cascading from the sky.

"Next tree!" declared Boris. "Quick!"

Hailey worked at top speed, and soon she'd carved snowflake patterns into all of Boris's trees. "I'd better go home now," she said as she turned to admire the last carved trunk.

"Hold on, there's just one more thing to do," said Boris, holding

up a piece of smooth bark that

had been gnawed into a diamond

shape. Hurriedly, Hailey pressed

her spines against it and moved in

the directions Boris told her.

"There," he said. "All done."

He held up the bark to show Hailey

and she saw that she'd carved a

beautiful star.

"Lovely!" she exclaimed.

"It's for you," Boris said. "To

thank you for all your help." He

hung it right in the middle of her

glowing leaf garland.

"Thank you!" cried Hailey.

"And now I must fly! Bye, Boris."

She made up her mind to go

straight home. "If I stop and pick

up any more leaves, I won't have
time to get ready for the parade,"
she said to herself.

Her red-and-silver wings
fluttered furiously as she sped
along. She raced past a tree
hung with balls of white-berried
mistletoe. It reminded her of the
decorations her mom was making,
and she flapped her wings harder.

Just as she was approaching
Dandelion Dell, she spotted some

69

leaves scattered messily on the
ground beneath a large oak tree.

"Oh, dear!" Hailey squeaked.
The parade would be coming this
way, and everyone would see them.
I'll pick them up quickly, she thought,
*then I'll rush straight home. I should
still be on time.*

Hurriedly, she flew down, then
curled up tight and began to roll
this way and that, gathering the
leaves. As soon as she started doing

70

her job she stopped worrying about being late and started singing her wintry song again:

> *I love winter when the wild wind*
> > *blows,*
> *Scattering the leaves all around,*
> > *all around,*
> *Even though it chills my nose*
> > *and toes,*
> *When I roll on the frosty ground.*

"How can you sing at a time like this?" a voice called from a

branch in the tree high above her.

Hailey stopped singing and uncurled quickly. "A time like what?" she replied, fluttering upward.

"A time as terrible and horrible and awful as this!" the voice wailed.

CHAPTER FIVE

Acorn Disaster!

Hailey flew closer. A beautiful silver Stardust Squirrel with cute tufty ears was crouched miserably on a branch, a broken basket beside her.

"Are you all right?" Hailey

asked anxiously.

"No," huffed the squirrel. "I

am actually all *wrong*!"

"Oh, dear." Hailey scratched her head with a tiny pink paw. "What's the matter?"

The squirrel sighed and twitched her bushy tail, sending a puff of glittery stardust into the air. "Are you sure you want to know?" she said, looking at Hailey and tilting her head to one side.

Hailey nodded.

"It's a very sad story. It's so sad it might even make you cry."

"Oh, er, that's all right," said Hailey bravely.

"Okay then." The squirrel clasped her front paws together. "Once upon a time, there was a very beautiful Stardust Squirrel called Sabrina—that's me," she added.

Hailey nodded and smiled.

"And one day—today, actually—Sabrina's mommy sent her out to fetch some acorns to decorate the delicious cake that

she's making for the Christmas Parade. So Sabrina did as she was told, because as well as being beautiful she's a very good little Stardust Squirrel. She filled her basket right to the brim. But then disaster struck!" Sabrina stared at her basket sadly. "Her basket broke and the acorns went all over the ground." Sabrina looked at Hailey. "Isn't that just the saddest story you've ever heard?"

Hailey nodded solemnly. "Yes, it is a very sad story," she said. "But maybe I can help you give it a happy ending."

Sabrina's eyes lit up. "How?"

Hailey fluttered over and examined the basket. It was woven from stems of dried grass, but some of them had broken and there was a hole in the bottom.

"Let's try putting some leaves over the hole," suggested Hailey.

"That might do the trick." She shook some leaves from her prickles, then carefully pressed a few on the bottom of the basket.

"Ooh, that looks a lot better," Sabrina said, twitching her tail

excitedly. "You can't see the hole at all now."

Hailey and Sabrina flew down to the ground. There were acorns scattered all over the grass, and they scampered around, picking them up and dropping them into the basket.

"Here goes," she said, lifting it.

For a moment it looked as though the repair was strong enough, but then the acorns and

leaves fell through the hole and rolled across the grass again.

"Oh no!" Sabrina groaned. "Now my story is going to have an even sadder ending than it did before!"

"Don't worry, I know how we can definitely make it happy," Hailey said.

Sabrina frowned at her. "How?"

"I'll collect them with my prickles. I'm sure they'll pick up

acorns just as well as they pick
up leaves from the ground."

Sabrina looked doubtful.
"There's an awful lot of them."

"Well, I've got an awful lot
of prickles!" Hailey giggled. She
curled into a ball and began to roll.
Soon all the acorns were stuck to
her prickles, along with the rest of
the fallen leaves.

"Come on, let's get these to
your mom," Hailey said. "We'll

have to hurry. The parade will be starting soon, and we mustn't miss it."

"Thank you!" Sabrina cried. "Now my story will have a very happy ending indeed!"

They flew at top speed through the trees, dodging between the branches. "There!" said Sabrina at last as a large nest came into view. It was made of sticks, dried grass, and leaves, and it was wedged into the fork where two branches joined

the trunk of a tall beech tree. They landed on a large branch.

"If you don't mind, I'll just put the acorns here," said Hailey. "I've got to go home to get ready."

"That will be great," Sabrina replied. "I can easily roll them into our nest from here."

Hailey shook her prickles. A few of the acorns came tumbling off, but most of them stayed put.

"Hang on, I'll get them off,"

said Sabrina. Grabbing an acorn, she pulled with all her might. "I'm not hurting you, am I, Hailey?"

Hailey could feel the tug on her spines but it wasn't sore. "No, it's okay, pull as hard as you can!"

Sabrina pulled and pulled and then, finally . . . *pop!* . . . the acorn came away from Hailey's spine.

"Hurray," cheered Hailey and Sabrina together.

"Now I *know* I'm strong

enough to get them off," said

Sabrina proudly. "I'll be as quick

as I can, so you're not late for the

parade." One by one, Sabrina

yanked the acorns from Hailey's

86

spines. "That's all of them!" she panted at last. "And a good thing, too. I'm puffed out!"

"Phew!" Hailey sighed with relief. "Now I must fly home as *fast* as my wings can take me!"

"Just a minute," Sabrina said as Hailey was about to flutter into the air. Sabrina flew above Hailey and flicked her tail. Twinkling silver stardust showered down on Hailey. "That's to say thank you

for helping me," Sabrina said with a smile.

"Wow!" Hailey gasped, twisting her head to look at her spines. They were twinkling like stars. "Thanks, Sabrina. That looks amazing!" Hailey flew up into the air. "See you at the parade," she called as she sped off through the trees. "If I get there in time . . ." she whispered to herself.

CHAPTER SIX

An Unexpected Guest

Hailey flew faster than she'd ever flown before. Misty Wood raced by in a blur, but at last she saw Hawthorn Hedgerows.

Zooming toward the ground,

she saw all the Hedgerow

Hedgehogs outside her burrow.

They were dressed in beautiful

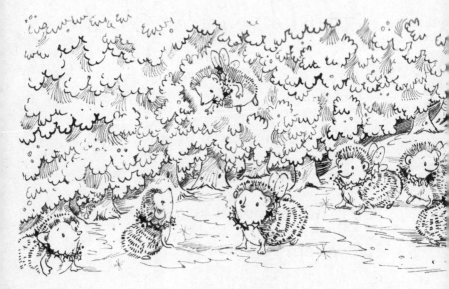

Zooming toward the ground,

she saw all the Hedgerow

Hedgehogs outside her burrow.

They were dressed in beautiful

90

garlands made of berries, acorns,

and golden leaves, ready for the

Christmas Parade.

Hailey's mom and dad were

among them, decked out in bright holly berries and mistletoe. They were looking around the crowd anxiously. Their eyes lit up in relief when they saw Hailey swishing through the air toward them.

"Where have you been?' Hailey's mom asked as she landed.

"Sorry," Hailey panted. "I had to help some friends and it made me late. Do I still have time to get dressed up for the parade?"

Suddenly, Hailey noticed that everyone was staring at her, their mouths gaping in astonishment. She began to feel a tiny bit worried.

"What's wrong?" she asked. She wondered if there was still an acorn or two stuck on her prickles.

"Nothing's wrong," her dad replied. "You look . . ."

"Wonderful!" her mom finished for him.

"Yes, you do," the other

hedgehogs agreed, crowding around
to see her better.

Hailey's neighbors Henry and
Hilda scurried into their burrow and
came back carrying an upturned
mushroom cap filled with water
that they used as a mirror. "Here,"
they said, setting it down in front of
Hailey. "Take a look at yourself."

Hailey peered at her reflection.
"Oh!" she gasped. Looking back
at her was a hedgehog whose fur

and prickles twinkled with silver stardust. Around her neck she wore a beautiful leafy garland that shone with pearly moonlight. A diamond-shaped piece of bark carved with a five-pointed star hung from it. Hailey stared and stared. She could hardly believe that the reflection was hers.

"That's the best Christmas costume I've ever seen!" Hailey's mom said, giving her a hug.

"We must go!" her dad cried.

"We don't want the parade to start
without us."

The hedgehogs took off, their wings glinting in the wintry sunshine. They flew fast, and soon they spotted Honeydew Meadow below them. A huge crowd of fairy animals was gathering there.

"Hurray!" cried Hailey. "We're not too late after all!"

Hailey, her mom and dad, and all their hedgehog friends fluttered to the ground and landed gently.

The Moss Mouse band was ready and waiting. Each mouse wore a lacy hat nibbled from a scarlet rosehip and, on their tails, a bow made from braided grass. They held their reed pipes and walnut shell drums ready to play. One tiny mouse started beating his drum eagerly as soon as he saw Hailey.

"Not yet, Morris," his mom whispered. "I'll tell you when to play."

"Hello, Moss Mice!" Hailey cried. "You all look so nice!" She could hardly wait for the music to begin.

Hailey's friend Bella the Bunny came hopping over. She was wearing a garland of white snowdrops around each long velvety ear and one around her neck. "Wow, you look fantastic, Hailey!" she cried.

"So do you," said Hailey.

She skipped around in a circle, too excited to keep still for even a moment.

Hailey heard some wings flapping above her head. She looked up eagerly and saw the Stardust Squirrels fluttering down. They were wearing garlands of polished nutshells and their fur shimmered with silver starlight. Hailey saw Sabrina and waved.

"Mom's Christmas cake looks

lovely—thanks to you," Sabrina called out to her.

Hailey grinned and puffed out her spikes proudly.

Next, the Cobweb Kittens arrived, their wings gleaming.

"Look at their costumes!" gasped Bella. The kittens wore garlands woven from glistening cobwebs and hung with bright, glimmering dewdrops.

"Everyone looks wonderful,"

101

Hailey said happily. "I'm so glad I got here in time."

Then the cheeky Pollen Puppies came scampering over, wagging their tails in excitement. "Whoo-hoo for the Christmas Parade!" they barked in chorus. "Whoo-hoo-woofy-whoo!"

Next, the Bark Badgers came marching past in a line, their silver wings neatly folded. Their black-and-white fur gleamed in the winter

sunshine, and they wore garlands made from beautifully carved bark shapes.

"And . . . halt!" cried the badger leader. They all stopped marching, and Hailey noticed Boris right at the back.

"Hi, Boris! How's your paw?" she called.

"Not too bad," he replied. "It won't stop me from being in the parade!"

Then the Holly Hamsters
arrived. Their golden fur shone
brightly, and around their necks
they wore garlands of crimson
holly berries.

Hugo came trotting over, grinning from ear to ear. "Just wait till everyone sees my holly bush," he whispered. "I bet they've never seen anything like it." His dark eyes widened suddenly. "Gosh," he said, stepping back and gazing at Hailey in astonishment. "You look beautiful, Hailey."

Hailey smiled. "Thanks, Hugo."

Finally, the Moonbeam Moles

appeared. They looked sleepy, but very happy to be there. Garlands of moonbeams hung around their necks, glowing like strings of pearls. Hailey looked over at Maisie and waved her paw. Maisie waved back with a snoozy smile.

Suddenly, the crowd fell silent. Hailey heard a gentle rustle from somewhere behind her. Turning, she saw an enormous bird flying toward Honeydew Meadow from

106

the Heart of Misty Wood. The bird had huge feathery wings that glinted gold in the sunshine. Her brown eyes were big and round and her beak was scarlet.

"Who's that?" asked Hugo and Bella together, looking up in wonder.

Hailey felt a great thrill of excitement and her heart began to thump. "I think . . . I think . . . it's the Wise Wishing Owl!" she gasped.

107

CHAPTER SEVEN

The Leader of the Parade

The Wise Wishing Owl was so
beautiful that Hailey could do
nothing but stare as she glided

down into the meadow and folded her vast wings. There was silence as the fairy animals waited for her to speak.

A smile spread slowly across the owl's face. "Is everybody ready for the Christmas Parade?" she called at last. Her voice tinkled like a waterfall splashing over rocks.

"Yes!" cried all the fairy animals together. They looked at one another in delight. The Wise

Wishing Owl, the oldest and most magical creature in Misty Wood, was hardly ever seen. This was a very special day indeed.

"Would you like to lead the parade, Your Wishingness?" asked one of the Bark Badgers.

The owl shook her feathery head. "Oh, no," she said. "One of you should take the lead. I have heard much of the Christmas Parade, and so I have come here to watch."

111

"Then will you do us the honor of *choosing* the leader for us?" asked the Bark Badger.

"Very well." The Wise Wishing Owl looked around at all the fairy animals, her snowy-white head turning slowly from side to side.

A shiver of delight ran through Hailey as the owl's gaze fell upon her. Never in her wildest dreams had she imagined that she would have the chance to look into the

deep brown eyes of the wonderful Wise Wishing Owl.

The owl furrowed her feathery brow. "It is not an easy choice," she said at last. "You all look very fine in your leaves and berries, your starshine and nutshells. But . . ." She stretched out a huge wing toward Hailey. "This little Hedgerow Hedgehog looks finer than anything I have ever seen. Will you lead the parade, my dear?"

Hailey gulped. She opened her mouth to reply, but no sound came out.

"Of course she will," squeaked

Bella, nodding at Hailey. "She would love to!"

Hailey took a deep breath. "Yes, I'd love to. Thank you, Wise Wishing Owl!" she cried.

"You are welcome," said the owl kindly.

"And you could start the parade off with your winter song, Hailey," Hugo piped up.

"Ooh, yes!" squealed Sabrina and Maisie.

All the fairy animals came crowding around. "We'd love to hear your song, Hailey," someone called out.

Hailey felt a tiny bit nervous, but she unfurled her wings and fluttered up above the other animals. Then she began to sing:

I love winter when the wild wind blows,

Scattering the leaves all around, all around,

Even though it chills my nose

and toes,

When I roll on the frosty ground.

As Hailey finished, her friends clapped and cheered. Hailey felt like she might burst with happiness. Then, chattering excitedly, all the fairy animals fluttered into line, ready for the Christmas Parade to begin.

The Hedgerow Hedgehogs scuttled to line up behind the

band. Behind them were the Bud
Bunnies and the Cobweb Kittens.
Then came the Holly Hamsters, the
Moonbeam Moles, and the Stardust
Squirrels. Behind the squirrels,
the Bark Badgers marched into
position. The Pollen Puppies were
right at the back, yapping excitedly
and running around in circles as
they waited for everyone to begin
moving.

"We're all ready!" cried Hailey

from high above. Light bounced off her beautiful garland and sparkled and danced all around Honeydew Meadow.

The Moss Mouse band began to play a marching song and Hailey felt her toes twitching in time to the music.

"I love winter!" she exclaimed as she headed to the front of the line. She was so happy that she did a forward roll, picking up a few

from high above. Light bounced off her beautiful garland and sparkled and danced all around Honeydew Meadow.

The Moss Mouse band began to play a marching song and Hailey felt her toes twitching in time to the music.

"I love winter!" she exclaimed as she headed to the front of the line. She was so happy that she did a forward roll, picking up a few

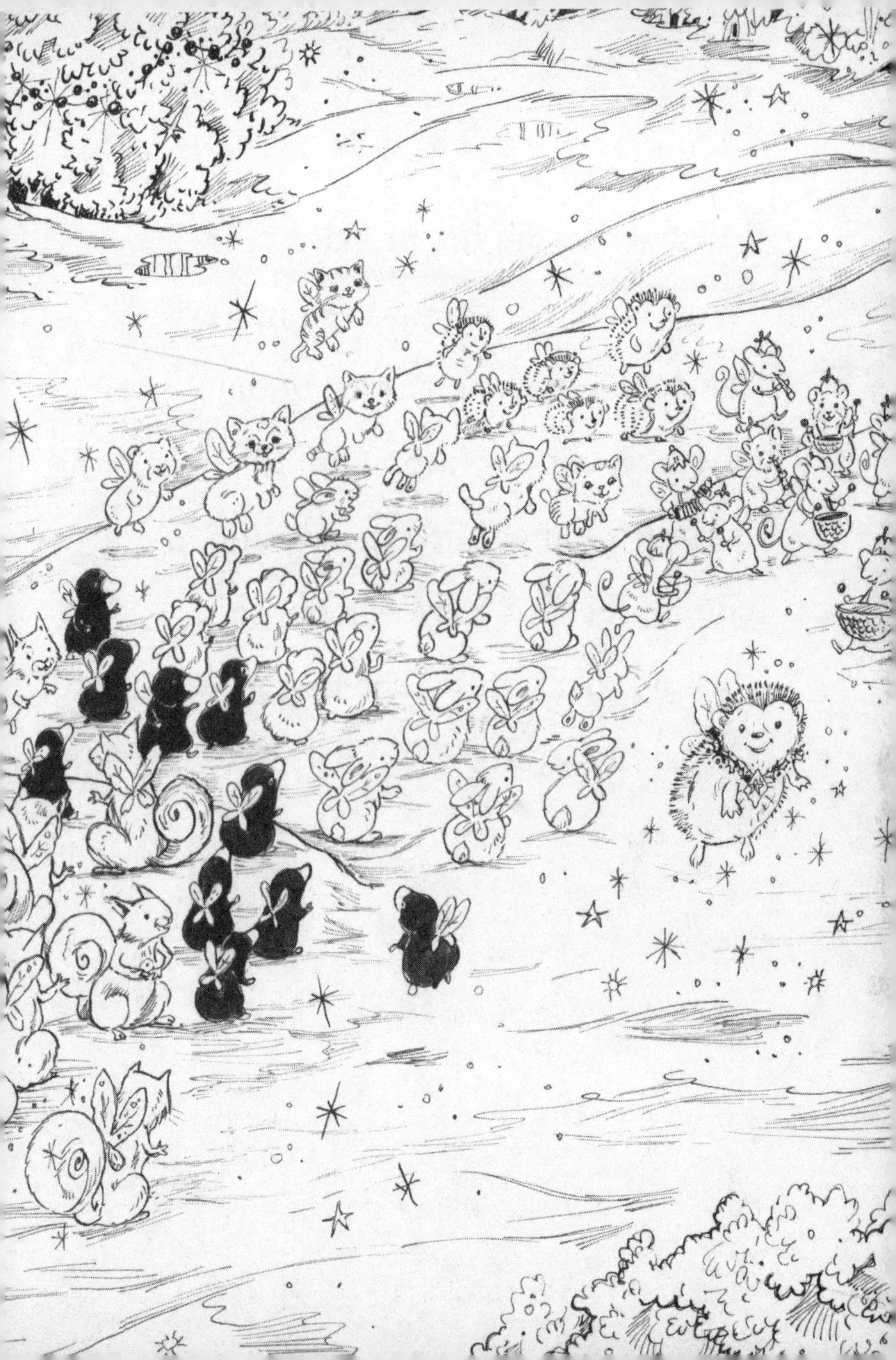

fallen leaves on her prickles.

"And I *love* Christmas even more!"
she called as she uncurled again.
She looked back happily at all
her fairy animal friends, waiting
eagerly behind her for the parade
to start. "And this is the best
Christmas ever!"

Turn the page for
lots of fun
Misty Wood
activities!

Connect the Dots

Follow the numbers and connect all the dots to make a lovely picture from the story. Start with dot number 1.

When you've finished connecting the dots, you can color the picture!

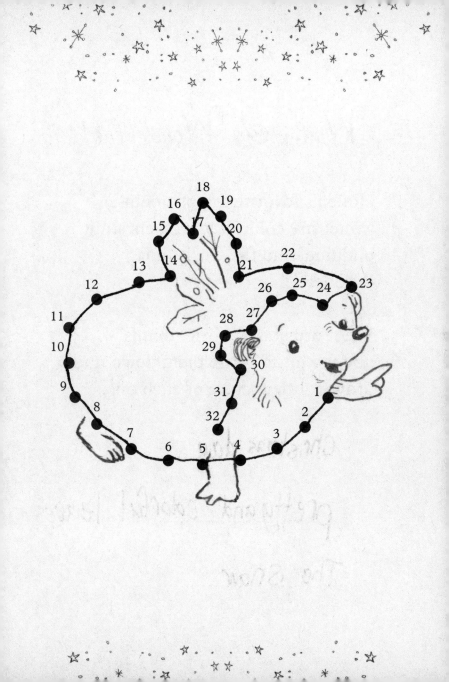

Winter Is Wonderful!

Hailey's favorite things about winter are colorful leaves, chestnut pudding, and the Christmas Parade!

What are your favorite things about winter? Write them down and draw a little picture of each one.

1. Christmas day

2. pretty and colorful leaves

3. The Snow

Help Hugo Remember!

Hugo the Holly Hamster likes Hailey's song so much *he* wants to sing it, too! But Hugo can't remember all the words. Can you help him? Give it a try without looking back at the story!

I love winter when the wild .wind...
    blows,
Scattering the .leaves. all around,
    all around,
Even though it chills my nose and
    .toes...,
When I roll on the frosty .ground

Fairy Animals

of Misty Wood

Meet more Fairy Animal friends!

Chloe the Kitten
Fairy Animals
of Misty Wood
Lily Small

Bella the Bunny
Fairy Animals
of Misty Wood
Lily Small

Mia the Mouse
Fairy Animals
of Misty Wood
Lily Small

Paddy the Puppy
Fairy Animals
of Misty Wood
Lily Small

Poppy the Pony
Fairy Animals
of Misty Wood
Lily Small